IT IS
MY TURN TO BE THE
LEADER

Written by Dr. Angela Jiles-Charles

Illustrated by Aljon Inertia

Published in the United States by J & C Publishing Corp.

jandcpublishingcorp.com

Library of Congress Cataloging-in-Publication Data is available upon request.

ISBN 978-1-7350532-0-2

DEDICATION

To Terrion Charles and Ronald Charles Jr., my loving children.

Thank you for such a great life raising the two of you.

You are my heart and I am very proud of you all.

The two of you are the best part of my life.

And to my nephew "Monty."

My love, may you rest in peace.

It was a beautiful spring day around noon. Isaiah and his younger sister, Tee, were inside the house watching television with Chunkie, their golden retriever.

Isaiah, being the oldest, always stepped up as the leader in everything he did with his sister. And Chunkie, who had a beautiful yellow coat, always spent his days with the two of them, waiting for someone to share their snacks, as they always did.

Well, the TV show was now finished, and Isaiah was getting a little bored. So, he looked around, trying to think of something to do.

Suddenly, an exciting idea came to him. He jumped up, and so did Chunkie, who was very excited, standing on his hind legs and bouncing around with Isaiah.

"Hey, Tee, let's go outside and play some soccer!" said Isaiah.

Tee liked the idea very much. "Sure, let's go. I will get the ball," she said.

"Okay!" Isaiah replied.

Both of them called out to Chunkie, who was wildly wagging his tail, hitting the two of them on their legs on the way out. Chunkie looked as if he was smiling with excitement.

"Soccer, yeah!" said Isaiah. "I am the leader!"

In the yard, Isaiah and Chunkie played with the ball, then Chunkie took the ball from Isaiah and ran around the yard.

Tee stood on the side watching Isaiah chase Chunkie through the leaves as they made a massive mess of the leaves, laughing and laughing.

"Look at those two!" Tee said.

After a while, Isaiah became tired from all the running, and he stopped chasing Chunkie.

Isaiah knelt on the ground, calling out to Chunkie, "Hey, big boy, come here," while slapping his hands on the ground. "Come here, big boy," Isaiah pleaded.

But Chunkie just kept running.

Seeing this, Tee knelt on the ground and called out to Chunkie while slapping her hands on the cool ground. "Come here, Chunk … Come, big boy!"

Chunkie stopped and looked at Tee. He paused with the ball in his mouth and then ran full speed toward her.

Chunkie ran so fast to Tee that he rolled her over, the ball still in his mouth. He jumped and playfully pounced on her while she laughed and laughed.

"Can I have the ball, man?" Tee took the ball from his mouth, and Chunkie let her take it. "Good boy. Thanks, Chunk!"

Isaiah called out, "Chunkie! I thought you were my buddy. Boys are supposed to stick together!"

Tee said, "No, that's not right." Tee dropped the ball to the ground. "I am the leader. I will kick the ball first!"

But before Tee could kick the ball, Isaiah called out, "Hold on a minute!"

He looked around, then said, "Tee, it doesn't matter who the leader is. But since we're talking about leaders, you know I play better than you."

He added, "Why do you want to be the leader? I think I am a better leader for soccer than you."

Tee said, "You always want to be the leader, and it is not fair."

She turned and started to walk away, passing by Chunkie, who was rolling around in the leaves.

Then she turned to Isaiah, saying, "Every time we are outside playing, even when we are playing with trucks, you are always first to be the leader."

Isaiah replied, "That is because I am good at being a leader at everything! Ha-ha! You want to race and see? I run faster than you, and I can kick the ball better because I am a boy!"

Tee said, "Just because you are a boy that does not make you better than girls."

She smiled and told Isaiah, "You might run faster, but I can kick just as good as you, and I am a girl. I am just as good as you."

She said, "Watch me! I have learned a new soccer trick. "I know how to kick the ball forward and turn my back to you fast and kick it with my back leg to someone else."

Tee demonstrated the trick.

"Ha-ha!" Isaiah laughed. "Yeah, I can do that trick too!"

"Hmmm?" Tee didn't believe him.

Isaiah thought about the trick, not sure if he could really do it. But one thing he knew—if he could not do the trick, Tee would never know! Isaiah was going to do his best showing Tee he could do her trick.

Isaiah tried to do the trick with the ball, but he slipped and almost fell to the ground. Oops! Fortunately, Desmond, their neighbor from next door, ran up and was able to catch him.

"Hey, guys, what are you doing?" Desmond asked. "You didn't look too sure about whatever you were trying to do," he added, clutching a couple of toy trucks.

"Desmond, did you see him? He looked funny, right? Isaiah was trying to do the new trick I learned. And he would have fallen to the ground if you had not caught him," Tee answered, laughing.

"Oooh, I wasn't going to fall … It was a trick! Ha-ha-ha!" Isaiah fibbed.

"Yeah? Well, okay, if you say so," Tee replied.

Desmond gave Chunkie a rub on the head, then he said, "When I saw you outside, I was curious, so I went out. Good thing I came at the right time."

"Well, Desmond, Tee wants to play soccer," said Isaiah. "And I want to be the leader if we play soccer because I can run faster than her."

"But I've been practicing this trick, and I can do it even if it's hard. It's so much fun, and I can show you how to do it. So, I should be the leader!" Tee said.

"It sounds like fun, but why don't we just play trucks? Hey, Isaiah, let's play trucks!" Desmond said, not really interested in soccer.

Tee turned to Desmond and said, "Desmond, we always play trucks with you. I want to play something else. Soccer is something else … And it's fun!"

Isaiah said, "Yeah, we know, but if you want to play soccer, I want to be the leader."

Desmond added, "And I want to play trucks."

"Boys, why do you always think you must be the leader?" Tee asked. "You know, I have ideas too. Good ideas!"

Tee thought out loud, "It would be nice if we have four players."

"Hey," Desmond said, "what about Chunkie? He's good at running with the ball!" He chuckled.

While Chunkie was still having his fun rolling in the leaves, Isaiah called out to him, "Come, big boy … Come this way."

Chunkie, with the ball in his mouth, stopped and looked at Isaiah, then ran toward him.

Before Chunkie reached Isaiah, Tee picked up a stick from the ground. Knowing how much Chunkie liked sticks, she waved it at him and said, "Hey, Chunk, let's trade!"

Chunkie, seeing the stick, turned away from Isaiah and ran in Tee's direction.

He dropped the soccer ball and took the stick then ran toward Isaiah.

"No, Chunkie! The ball, not the stick!" Isaiah said, hitting his forehead with his palm in frustration.

Tee and Desmond stood there laughing while holding their tummies. It was so funny! But Desmond didn't care because he really wanted to play with the trucks he brought out with him.

Chunkie went back and grabbed the ball again with his mouth and ran fast toward Isaiah.

Isaiah tried to defend the goal, but Chunkie was too fast, and Tee was cheering Chunkie all the way. "Yeah! Go, Chunkie!" Tee yelled while jumping in the air.

Chunkie was running very fast and finally scored a goal.

Overjoyed and laughing, she told Isaiah, "Ha-ha-ha! See? I have good ideas too."

Although Chunkie scored for her, Isaiah still did not want Tee to be the leader. "Well, I have been playing longer, and I know other tricks too," he said.

Desmond added, "Well, I just like trucks. I like trucks!"

Tee explained, "I know you have played soccer longer, Isaiah. And I know that you like trucks, Desmond, but we can do something other than that today."

Isaiah seemed not as interested in playing soccer if he was not the leader, Tee thought. So, she smiled and walked away from the boys, calling out to Chunkie, "Come on, boy. Let's go play soccer."

Desmond called out, "Hey, where are you going, Tee? I know both of you can play, but what about trucks? Oh my, trucks are so much fun! And we can be leaders for our trucks and have fun!"

"Desmond, if you had your own truck company, would you let me drive your truck? I think driving trucks would be fun too!" Tee asked.

"Well, Tee, I'll let you after you learn how to drive a truck," Desmond answered.

"Thanks, Desmond, because when I'm older, I can sure learn how to drive a truck if I want to," Tee said.

"Girls can do anything, Desmond," she added.

"When I grow up, I am going to be anything I want to be. Just like we had a black president, we will have a lady president. Maybe even me!"

"You? What do you mean, Tee?" Desmond asked.

"Maybe I will be a president," replied Tee.

"How do you know you can be a lady president?" Isaiah asked.

"I know because girls are smart, kind, and strong!" Tee said proudly. "I am going to start a business when I am older and I can be a lady president, Isaiah," Tee told her brother.

"Well, Tee, I am going to start my own company and I can become the president too," Isaiah said.

"That's good, Isaiah, because we both can be whatever we want to be," Tee replied.

"Just like boys, girls have great ideas too. We have a voice to express ourselves, and many people will listen to us. We can do what boys can do, sometimes even better!" she said with a smile.

"When girls are given the same chances, we can also be doctors, lawyers, judges, janitors, teachers, and engineers … and truck drivers!" she added.

Then Tee said, "But today, I want to be the leader of our soccer game and play soccer, kicking the ball and running with you two and Chunkie! It is my turn to be the leader. Are you going to follow me as your leader? Come on and let's have some fun!"

NEW WORDS*

leader (noun). A person who has commanding authority or influence

idea (noun). A plan for action

demonstrate (verb). To show clearly

clutch (verb). To grasp or hold with or as if with the hand usually strongly, tightly, or suddenly

practice (verb). To train by repeated exercises

trade (verb). To give one thing in exchange for another

express (verb). To represent usually in words

really (adverb). Used to emphasize

fair (adjective). Not biased; honest

* Definitions are taken from Merriam-Webster.com.

CAREER WORDS IN THE STORY

president	doctor	lawyer	judge
janitor	teacher	engineer	truck driver

FOOD FOR THOUGHT

Do you think Tee should be a leader playing soccer?

Why do you think it is okay to take turns being the leader?

Girls are smart and strong, and we can do several things really well.

Tell us what you like doing.

Go to our webpage and let us know what you like doing and share pictures!

I would love to see what you and your siblings like doing.

Dr. Angela Jiles-Charles

Made in the USA
Columbia, SC
29 June 2020